LINDSAY CAMP

CABBAGES FROM OUTER SPACE

ILLUSTRATED BY TONY ROSS

RED FOX

A Red Fox Book

Published by Random House Children's Books
20 Vauxhall Bridge Road, London SW1V 2SA

A division of Random House UK Ltd
London Melbourne Sydney Auckland
Johannesburg and agencies thoughout the world

Copyright © text Lindsay Camp 1994
Copyright © illustrations Tony Ross 1994

1 3 5 7 9 10 8 6 4 2

First published by Andersen Press Ltd 1994

Red Fox edition 1995

Printed and bound in Great Britain by
The Guernsey Press Co. Ltd, Guernsey, Channel Islands.
RANDOM HOUSE UK Limited Reg. No. 954009

ISBN 0 09 942771 0

Contents

1
Game Crazy

Emma was crazy about computer
games.

She played them at school on the
class computer. She played them at
home on her mum's computer.

And when her mum was using her computer, Emma went round the corner to her best friend Rebecca's, and played games on her television set.

Emma's mum and dad used to moan about it all the time.

'Why don't you play your recorder instead?' said her mum. 'You were getting so good before you stopped practising.'

'Don't feel like it,' said Emma.

'Or you could draw a picture,' said her dad.

'Or read a book,' said her mum.

'Or take your bike out on the
pavement,' said her dad.

'No thanks,' said Emma. 'Computer games are more exciting.'

2
The MiniMax

Then, just after Emma's birthday, her Uncle Richard came to stay.

He'd just come back from America, and he brought her the most fantastic present.

It was a MiniMax Double-X
Personal Entertainment System.

It was small enough to take anywhere. It had earphones, so you could hear all kinds of exciting noises. And it came with three different games: Wobblyworld, The Evil Thargons, and Cabbages from Outer Space.

'Wow!' said Emma, rushing up to her room to experiment with it.

The first game she tried was
Cabbages from Outer Space. It was
brilliant.

She played it before she got out of
bed in the morning.

She played it in the bathroom,

and while she was having her breakfast.

She played it on the way to school,
and on the way home.

She played it when she went to the
supermarket with her dad,

and when she went to her
grandparents' house for tea.

In fact, the only times she didn't play
it were when she was in class, and
when she was asleep.

And then she dreamed about it.

Emma's parents moaned even more.

'You can't play with that thing all
the time,' said her dad.

'I said you can't play with that thing
all the time,' he repeated, pulling up
Emma's earphones so she would hear
him.

'Why not?' said Emma.

'Because there are so many better things to do in life,' said her mum.

'Not in my life there aren't,' said Emma. 'Computer games are more exciting than anything that ever happens to me.'

And she clamped her earphones firmly back on.

3
Level One

After school that day, Emma went round to Rebecca's house.

It was a beautiful sunny afternoon, and they played for quite a while in the tree-house that Rebecca's mum and dad had built in the garden.

Then they went inside to play
computer games on the television set.
'I was just going to bring you a sna
in the tree-house,' said Rebecca's m
But the girls didn't even hear he

Soon, it was time for Emma to go home for supper. It was only a couple of minutes' walk, but she turned on her MiniMax anyway.

She hadn't played Cabbages from Outer Space since before school.

As she kicked Rebecca's front gate ꜱed behind her, Emma was on ͏ 1.

She was concentrating so hard on steering the space shuttle through the asteroid shower that she didn't look up from her screen for a second.

And with the sound turned up lo~~ she didn't hear anything strange either.

4
Level Two

vel 2 was harder, so Emma leaned
st a lamp-post for a moment to
re her hands were steady.

Captain Urg was getting closer.
Emma dodged – first to the left, then
to the right.

It was very strange, but suddenly her feet felt heavy, almost as if they were stuck to the ground . . .

With one last twist, Emma left Urg
and his space bandits behind.

Bleepa-bleepa bleep, buh-buh-buh
bleeeeep! She was onto Level 4.

6
Level Four

Emma had landed safely on Urgold VI.
 Now the game started to get really
difficult. And to make things even
harder, everything seemed to be
shaking up and down.

 Emma wondered if it could be an
earthquake in Laburnum Drive, but
she wasn't going to look up at a
moment like this . . .

Emma clung on to the MiniMax's
controls as tightly as she could.

Now she had to send a search party to the Carcassadian Caves to hunt for the Sonic Shredder, while using her foot-soldiers to guard the Cosmic Cabbage from Urgold Super-Caterpillars.

It needed maximum concentration.

The shaking was getting worse. It
must definitely be an earthquake,
thought Emma.

And she knew she should run home
to make sure her family were all right.
But she couldn't stop playing now –
not just when she was about to find
the Sonic Shredder . . .

7
Level Five

The earthquake seemed to be over –
and Emma had the Sonic Shredder.

She'd only reached Level 5 twice
before. Her hands trembled with
excitement.

If she could just shred the Cosmic
Cabbage fast enough . . .

Emma finished shredding the first quarter of the cabbage.

'Yes!' she cried aloud – and then she remembered that she was in Laburnum Drive, and hoped that no one had heard her.

But she wasn't going to look up from her screen, not with three-quarters of the cabbage left to shred.

'Yes!' shouted Emma again, as she finished shredding the second quarter . . .

The third quarter was done. And once more, Emma felt the strange quiver-y feeling inside.

Her legs went all wobbly too – but then, they always did when she was really excited.

Emma finished shredding.
Bleep blip-blip-blip bleep bleep
bleeeeeep! The MiniMax played a
fanfare.

Emma had done it! She'd made the Cosmic Coleslaw, just in time.

She was onto Level 6.

She was so delighted she leapt high into the air . . .

8
Level Six

Now all Emma had to do was feed the
Cosmic Coleslaw to the Good Wizard
Warburton, to restore his faded
powers, and the Universe would be
saved.

Suddenly, she felt an even stranger
feeling than before – a sort of rushing,
whizzing, trembly, falling-to-pieces
feeling – but nothing was going to stop
her now.

One spoonful . . . two spoonfuls . . .
the strange feeling seemed to have
passed . . . three spoonfuls . . . Wizard
Warburton had finished all the
Cosmic Coleslaw.

Bleepety bleepety bleep bleep
bleepety blip-blip blippa-blippa
bleeeeeeeeeeep! The MiniMax went
mad. Wizard Warburton's powers
returned, and the Universe was safe.

Emma had scored the maximum
possible.

She knew she should be pleased, but the funny thing was she felt a little disappointed.

What was she going to do now?

She supposed she could try playing Wobblyworld or The Evil Thargons instead – but somehow she felt as if she already knew what they would be like. It was almost as if she had played them before . . .

Emma looked up from her screen, and saw she was right outside her own front door.

To her relief, the house didn't seem to have been damaged by the earthquake.

She pulled off her earphones and hurried up the path, hoping she wasn't too late for supper.

That night, going upstairs to say
goodnight to Emma, her mum heard
a strange noise coming from her room.
It wasn't the usual bleep-bleep-
bleepety-bleeping of the MiniMax . . .

As her mum came into the room,
Emma put her recorder under her
pillow and snuggled down ready for
sleep.

Her mum sat down on the edge of the bed.

'Mum,' said Emma, 'do you know what I did today on the way home from Rebecca's?'

'No,' said her mum, kissing her. 'What?'

'I saved the Universe,' said Emma.

'You and that machine,' said her mum, smiling.

'Do you think you and dad could build me a tree-house like Rebecca's?' said Emma.